Drop Everything, It's D.E.A.R. Time!

by Ann McGovern
Illustrated by Anna DiVito

SCHOLASTIC INC.

New York Toronto London Auckland Sydney

For Sharon Jane Mulligan, who inspired this book.
And for all the girls and boys – and their wonderful
teachers and principals – who have D.E.A.R TIME in their schools.
– A.M.

For Joan
– A.D.

ISBN 0-590-45802-7

Text copyright © 1993 by Ann McGovern.
Illustrations copyright © 1993 by Anna DiVito.
All rights reserved. Published by Scholastic Inc.

12 11 10 9 8 7 6 5 4 3 2 1   3 4 5 6 7 8/9

Printed in the U.S.A.   09

First Scholastic printing, January 1993

It's a day like any other school day.

Mrs. Freeman's class is making stone soup.
Dennis puts carrots into the soup and asks,
"Is it *dear time* yet?"

Mr. Wong's class is learning about life in the sea.
Chris is a scuba diver.
"When will it be *dear time*?" he asks.

Ms. Angeli's class is sailing on the *Mayflower*.
Sharon pretends to be seasick and she throws up,
just like some of the Pilgrims did.
"Now is it *dear time*?" she asks.

Miss Mulligan's class is putting on a play
about presidents.
José is George Washington,
but his wig is too big.
"When is *dear time* coming?" he asks.

In the music room, there's drumming
and strumming, fluting and tooting.
Mr. Garcia needs earplugs!

In the gym, there's bumping and bouncing.

In the art room, Annie paints a picture,
and John works with mushy clay.

In the kitchen, cooks are baking pies.

In the principal's office, Mr. Charles is scolding Jimmy.

In the basement,
Mr. Martin is fixing
a leaky pipe.

In the library, books
are falling off shelves.

In the science room,
a volcano erupts.

In the computer lab,
Pete puts in the
wrong disk.

In the nurse's room,
Nurse Tamika bandages
Odile's arm.

Yes, it's a busy school day, just like any other.
Until . . .

. . . drop everything — it's D.E.A.R. time!

Drop Everything And Read time!

Grab a book time.

While the stone soup simmers, Mrs. Freeman's students grab their picture books.

While the sharks open their mighty jaws,
Mr. Wong's students stick their noses
in their books.

While the *Mayflower* sails away,
Ms. Angeli's class reads.

While José's wig falls off,
Miss Mulligan's students hide behind their books.

In the music room, no more fluting and tooting.
Mr. Garcia takes out his earplugs.

In the gym, no more bumping and bouncing.

In the art room, pictures go unpainted, and clay gets hard.

The cooks stop baking.

The principal stops scolding.

The janitor stops fixing.

The librarian stops sorting.

The volcano stops smoking.

The computer goes berserk.

Nurse Tamika stops bandaging.

It's D.E.A.R. time for everyone.

DROP EVERYTHING AND READ TIME!

And the very best thing . . .

...is that it will happen again tomorrow...

...and tomorrow...

. . . and tomorrow.